MAY IS FOR MACK

MOUNTAIN MEN OF MUSTANG MOUNTAIN

DYLANN CRUSH

EVE LONDON

To the Match of the Month Patrons, especially...

Jackie Ziegler

And to our Kickstarter supporters, especially...

Natasha Tucker, *who named Triton!*

Thank you so much for your support. We couldn't do what we love without you!

Dear Reader,

Thanks for picking up a copy of May is for Mack, book five in the Mountain Men of Mustang Mountain series! We can't wait for you to meet Mack and Lily. If you love their story and want to learn more about Mustang Mountain, sign up for our newsletter here: http://subscribepage.io/MatchOfTheMonth.

XOXO,
Dylann & Eve

May is for Mack

Will love be enough to save this scarred mountain man?

Lily

I've got one goal: build my catering business up to the point where I never have to worry about money again. It's been my sole focus since the day I took on my first job. My friends say they understand my ambition, but none of them have ever worried about where their next meal might come from.

Then I meet him.

Scarred and broken, he's a shell of a man. I know what it feels like to live in that dark place where not even the brightest light can reach.

I don't need to rescue him—he's more than capable of doing that himself. But sticking around to help him save himself would mean risking everything.

Mack

My life might not be ideal, but it's fine. I have everything I need in Mustang Mountain. At least I thought I did until I met her. Being around Lily is like circling the sun. She makes me ache for a life I don't deserve.

When we're forced to work on a fundraiser together, I start to think maybe there's a chance for us. But will she be able to see past my scars when she realizes they're not just skin deep?

Welcome to Mustang Mountain where love runs as wild as the free-spirited horses who roam the hillsides. Framed by rivers, lakes, and breathtaking mountains, it's also the place the Mountain Men of Mustang Mountain call home. They might be rugged and reclusive, but they'll risk their hearts for the curvy girls they love.

CHAPTER 1

MACK

I DIDN'T HAVE time to go all the way into town this afternoon to meet Ruby, but somehow, I could never say no to her. None of the guys who lived on Mustang Mountain could. She might be annoying as hell sometimes and stick her nose into places where it definitely didn't belong, but she was as much a part of Mustang Mountain as the landscape itself.

Before I took off, I needed to check on my new hire. Caden had only been working with me for a few weeks but seemed to have a good handle on what needed to be done. I ducked into one of the outbuildings on my property where I kenneled the sled dogs, who were just about ready to breed. I was already behind schedule this spring. If we didn't get these females bred soon, we might as well forget about it this season.

"Hey, boss." Caden looked up as I entered. He was my MC brother Shaw's younger brother, and I'd taken him under my wing in an effort to keep him out of trouble. "I think you need to take a look at Persephone before we match her up with Triton."

"What makes you think that?" Persephone was only three years old, but she'd been one of my best sled dogs over the winter. Even a mention that there might be something wrong with her made my stomach roll.

"It's nothing bad. She's just acting a little funny," Caden said.

"It will have to wait. I've got to run into town for a while, and I'm not sure when I'll be back. You think you can finish up around here on your own this afternoon?"

"Yeah, I can do that." Caden's chest puffed out a bit.

The kid had been doing a good job and deserved to take on some additional responsibilities. He reminded me of one of the recruits I'd trained back when I worked as a firefighter in Texas. I hadn't thought about my time there in a while. There was no use since I couldn't go back and change the past. I pushed the memories that threatened away and refocused on Caden.

"Good. Everything that needs to be done is on the list. Make sure you lock up the office when you leave and keep an eye out for Hades." The big wolf was more town mascot than wild animal, but he could tell it was breeding season, and I'd caught him sniffing around a lot more than usual over the past several days.

"Will do. Don't worry about a thing. I've got it all under control." Caden gave me a cocky grin.

I shook my head before I walked out the door, hoping like hell I hadn't misplaced my trust in him. I'd done that with someone else once, and it had almost cost me everything.

A half-hour later, I pulled my baseball cap down low and pushed through the doors of the Nelson Mercantile. Ruby didn't say exactly what she needed, only that it had to do with some event she wanted to pull together at the last minute that would give me a chance to raise awareness about mushing.

I'd only been living in Mustang Mountain for a few years, but I'd already learned that when Ruby got a wild hair up her ass, it was better to get involved at the start. Otherwise, she'd make her own plans and expect everyone else to rearrange their lives to conform to her wishes.

I lifted a hand and waved at her husband, Orville, who was working behind the front counter. He was also the mayor, but folks around here didn't bother to put on airs. Ruby stood at the back of the store, one hand gripping a carafe of coffee and the other already reaching for a mug.

"Hey, Mack. Thanks for stopping by." She set the mug down in front of me and filled it with the strong-smelling brew.

"It didn't seem like I had much of a choice," I said, only halfway joking. "What's so important that it couldn't wait a few days?"

She put the carafe back on the warmer and leaned against the counter. "You're a few minutes early. I'd rather wait until everyone's here to go over the details, so I only have to do it once."

"What are you talking about? Who else is coming?" My jaw immediately clenched. I hated being caught off guard. She hadn't said anything about this being a group project.

"Well, we can't very well have an event without refreshments." Ruby smiled at someone behind me. "Here she comes now."

I knew what she was up to before I turned around. Damn her for setting herself up to be some self-appointed Cupid.

Ruby patted a spot on the counter to my left. "Lily, I'm so glad you could make it. Come sit down next to Mack so I can fill the two of you in on what I have in mind."

I turned slightly, just far enough to get a good look at the woman I hadn't been able to get out of my mind. We met last month at the Easter egg hunt my MC club had helped put on at the mustang refuge. Lily was everything I could ever want in a woman. She ran her own successful catering business and had a need to succeed that rivaled my own. Pair that with glossy black hair reaching all the way down her back to skim the top of her heart-shaped ass, and big blue eyes rimmed with full, dark lashes, and I'd fallen for her in the space of a single afternoon.

"Any chance you've got a cup of coffee for me,

Ruby?" She slid onto the stool next to me and held out her hand. "Mack, it's good to see you again. Or maybe I should say it's good to finally see you, since you were wearing a bunny suit the first time we met."

Just hearing her voice sent heat racing through my veins. If I took her hand, I might not be able to ever tear myself away. Why had Ruby put me in an impossible situation? I kept my head turned so Lily couldn't see the right side of my face. The scars didn't bother me anymore, but I didn't want to witness her reaction when she saw them for the first time.

"I don't want to be rude, but I just remembered I need to pick up an order at the bakery before they close." It was a lame excuse, but the best I could do under the circumstances. Pulling the collar of my jacket up to hide my cheeks, I glared at Ruby. "I'm sorry to run out on you both like this. I'll follow up with you tomorrow, Ruby."

Ruby's shoulders slumped in defeat. "I'm sure Orville would be happy to run over and get that for you, Mack."

I was already halfway to the door and had no intention of turning around. "I'll call you in the morning," I tossed over my shoulder before I escaped through the front door.

The cool spring air hit my face as I stepped out onto the sidewalk, and I gulped in a huge breath. I'd managed to avoid Lily for the past few weeks, but I wouldn't be able to keep it up forever, especially now that Ruby was involved.

She got lucky when Jackson, Ford, Miles, and Asher fell in love, and didn't see anything wrong with taking the credit. If she thought she could make me into the next Mustang Mountain bachelor, she was dead wrong. She might think a woman like Lily would be able to see past my scars, but she had no idea exactly how deep they ran.

"I'M SORRY, SUGAR." Ruby cocked her hip and stared after Mack. "I didn't mean to waste your time this afternoon."

My shoulders slumped in disappointment. I'd been looking forward to seeing Mack again. We'd hit it off at the Easter egg hunt the Mustang Mountain Riders had hosted last month. When Ruby asked if I'd be willing to take part in a last-minute women's weekend event involving Mack's sled dogs, I couldn't say yes quickly enough. Especially since she wanted to donate a portion of the profits to the local women's shelter. Evidently, he didn't feel the same way about working with me.

"It's okay." I wrapped my hands around the mug and lifted it to my lips. "It's been a slow week, and I'd never turn down a cup of your coffee. One of these days, you need to tell me where you get it. It's the best-kept secret in Mustang Mountain."

Ruby flushed at the compliment. "He'll come around. Mack's always taken a long time to warm up to new people."

"That's just it... I'm not new. We spent the better part of an entire afternoon at the Easter egg hunt together." I shook my head. It was probably for the best that he spooked. There was no room in my life for a man, especially not one who made my blood heat just by the sound of his gruff, deep voice.

"I'll follow up with him. If we're going to pull that event together, he's going to need to get on board sooner rather than later. Or,"—Ruby slapped her hand on the counter and leaned toward me—"maybe you'd be willing to stop by and see him on your way home."

I laughed at the suggestion. "You know as well as I do that Mack's place isn't exactly on my way home."

Ruby's eyes sparkled. "But you said yourself that it's been a slow week. Sounds like you might have the time."

She had me there. I'd grown up outside of Mustang Mountain and had known Ruby almost all my life. One of these days I might wise up enough to beat her at her own game, or at least see her coming before she had me pigeon-holed.

"Tell you what. Give me a to-go cup of your coffee and we'll call it a deal?"

She pulled a thick paper cup out from her stash under the counter and filled it to the brim. "There you go. Let me know what he says."

Forty-five minutes later, I pulled into a gravel drive

halfway up the mountain. I hadn't been to the kennels before, though I'd driven past them multiple times. I was surprised Mack, and I hadn't met before the Easter egg hunt last month since he'd moved to Mustang Mountain a few years ago. The rumor mill always circulated when someone new settled in town. From what I'd heard, he liked to keep to himself. Most folks speculated it was because of his scars.

Though I hadn't seen them in person yet, I knew he'd been injured on the job when he was a firefighter back in Texas. If they were as bad as people said, I didn't blame him for being a little shy around strangers.

I got out of the car and pulled my jacket over my shoulders. It always amazed me how the temperature could be a dozen degrees lower up here. And with the way the wind picked up this high on the mountain, it almost felt like winter hadn't quite given up its grip.

It was almost five. Maybe I should have waited until tomorrow to try to catch Mack at work. He lived on the property, but I didn't want to bother him at home. I headed toward the closest building, hoping he was like me and didn't adhere to regular business hours. Being self-employed, there was no such thing as a forty-hour work week.

The door squeaked open as I stepped inside a large, insulated outbuilding that appeared to double as the sled dog office. Lights blazed overhead and the soft sound of country music came through a doorway behind the counter.

"Hello?" I raised my voice so that it might be heard

over the music. When no one responded, I ventured behind the desk and glanced down the hall. Another doorway led out to an area that looked like it might house some of the dogs. I was about to venture that way to see if I could find Mack when he opened the door and stepped through.

"Oh. Hey, Lily." His dark eyes widened in surprise before he turned the right side of his face away from me. "I didn't hear you come in."

My heart rattled inside my rib cage. "I'm sorry. I called out but wasn't sure if anyone could hear me over the music."

Mack immediately reached for the dial on the vintage boom box and turned it down. "Sorry about that. I guess I'm used to being the only one around this time of day."

Neither one of us could move very much without bumping into the other in the narrow space. I was sure he'd be able to see my pulse pounding if he came any closer.

"Why don't we go back out front, and you can tell me what brought you halfway up the mountain?" Mack gestured toward the door behind me.

Sensing he was eager to increase the distance between us, I retreated. "Ruby asked me to check in on my way home. Since we don't have much time to figure out the details of the women's weekend, she thought it would make sense to get started right away."

"Of course, she'd think that." He put his palms on the counter as I stepped around to the other side. "I don't know how well you know Ruby, but I think she might have an ulterior motive for getting us to work together."

I was well aware of Ruby's matchmaking efforts—me and everyone else within about a hundred-mile radius of Mustang Mountain. "Don't tell me you're her Mister May?"

"Evidently. She thinks she's on a roll, but her streak will end with me." He lifted his head, and I got my first real look at the scars covering the right side of his face.

I knew he'd been burned, but hearing about it and seeing the aftermath with my own eyes were two completely different things. His skin stretched taut over his cheek and down his neck like it had been melted. My chest squeezed tight as I quickly looked away.

Hoping he hadn't witnessed my reaction, I tried to nail him down about the event. "Should we talk about the women's weekend? Ruby said she was hoping to incorporate an outdoor picnic with a demo of your sled dog team afterward."

He glanced past me, unwilling to make eye contact. "I need to check on the dogs. If you don't mind talking while we walk, you're more than welcome to come along."

Shame flooded through my system. I wished I could snap my fingers and get a do-over so I could better mask my reaction. Instead, I forced a too-bright smile and pulled the small notebook I always carried with me out of my purse. "That would be great. Lead the way."

He grabbed a jacket off a hook behind him and tugged it on before he held the door for me to go outside. "It's easier if we drive over to the kennels. You okay with taking my truck?"

"Sure." He opened the door, and I climbed up onto the big bucket seat.

He crossed in front of the grill, then got behind the wheel. "You might want to buckle up. The road can be a little bumpy this time of year with all the snowmelt."

With my seatbelt fastened in place, he fired up the engine and navigated the truck away from the building. Branches scraped at the roof as we started down a narrow, muddy road.

"How many dogs do you have out here?" I'd watched sled dog races like Montana's Race to the Sky from afar, but had never gotten up close to the dogs.

"About twenty-five right now, though we're getting into breeding season." He kept his eyes trained on the road ahead, but I was too self-conscious to take the opportunity to study his profile.

"What does that entail?"

"Breeding dogs?" He shot a quick glance in my direction. "I suppose it entails what you'd expect. We figure out which pair we'd like to breed, put them together, and let Mother Nature take care of the rest."

Heat marched across my cheeks, but I continued, undeterred. "I bet the puppies are cute."

"Yeah, they really are." His voice softened with

that last statement, giving me hope that I hadn't completely ruined our fragile friendship. "You ready to meet some of the dogs?"

"Sure."

He brought the truck to a stop, and I looked through the front windshield. A low building sat to one side with chain link fencing separating individual dog runs. Small dog houses dotted the clearing in front of us. It looked like an entire village. Dozens of dogs yipped, barked, and strained at their leads as we got out of the truck.

"They get a little excited for visitors." Mack slowed down to match my stride.

A flash of gray caught my eye at the edge of the clearing. The biggest dog I'd ever seen ran right through the middle of the village of dog houses.

"Why isn't that one on a lead?" I followed his progress toward the kennel, awed by the grace in his movements.

"Because that's not one of my dogs. That's a wolf."

I ALWAYS SEEMED to forget that folks who didn't live in Mustang Mountain might not know about Hades.

Lily grabbed my arm. "A wolf?"

"Yeah, he's like the town mascot. Come here, Hades." I held my hand out toward the big gray wolf. He trotted over and rubbed his giant head against it. "You can pet him if you want. Just let him sniff your hand first."

Her grip on my arm tightened as she slowly slid her other hand out of her pocket for Hades to examine. He wrinkled his nose, then nuzzled his muzzle into her side.

"Most folks around here would rather shoot a wolf than try to tame it," she said.

"Most folks aren't like Jackson Hill. He found Hades when the wolf was just a pup and couldn't fend for himself. Now he hangs around town and goes where he pleases. As long as he doesn't cause any trouble, everyone seems content to leave him alone." Seemed like a good life to me. The kind of life I'd been looking for when I left Texas for the remote mountains of Montana.

"And he doesn't bother the dogs at all?" Lily let go of my arm so she could scratch between Hades's ears.

"Not in the way you might think. He and the team leads have a mutual respect for each other, though he can be a pain in the ass when the females are in heat."

Hades shook his head, evidently done being the center of attention, then trotted over to the kennel on the end. The one housing Persephone. A knot of apprehension tightened in my gut. I'd need to keep an eye on him if I didn't want to end up with a litter of wolf-dog pups running around.

Lily followed me as I checked on the dogs and made sure they had fresh water. I introduced her to them all by name and she seemed to enjoy hearing about some of our trials on the trails. By the time we were done making the rounds, the sun had started to slip beyond the horizon, and she hadn't said another word about the event Ruby wanted us to plan.

Being with her made me lose track of time. Except for her initial pause when she first saw my scars, she hadn't treated me any differently than she did the afternoon we met. Though my face had been hidden by the damn Easter bunny mask my MC brothers had talked me into wearing, Lily and I hadn't had any trouble keeping the conversation flowing. This afternoon was the same. I was surprised to realize I was actually enjoying myself for a change.

"I suppose we'd better put some thought into Ruby's women's weekend idea," Lily said as I stopped the truck in front of the office.

There it was—the reminder of why Lily had sought me out. While we'd been visiting the dogs, I'd let myself pretend that she might actually be enjoying the conversation as much as I had. The whole time she'd probably been trying to figure out a way to turn the conversation back to Ruby's event. I felt like a fool for wasting her time.

"Sorry, I get a little carried away talking about the dogs. You're probably starving and ready to head home after such a long day. Just tell me what you and Ruby need, and I'll see what I can do."

As if on cue, her stomach growled. She covered her belly with her palm. "I guess I am a little hungry. I've got a few groceries in the cooler in the back of my car that I picked up in town. It would only take me a few minutes to whip up something for us to eat if you want to talk over dinner."

"Dinner?"

A shy smile spread across her lips as she glanced down at her hand. "I suppose it's pretty presumptuous of me to invite myself over for dinner. You're right. I should get going."

"You want to make me dinner?" Saying it out loud didn't make it sound less strange. "At my place?"

Her lashes fluttered against her cheeks. "With an

invitation like that, how could I refuse? I can make a quick pasta dish. Just let me grab a few things I need from my car."

I heard what she said. I just couldn't comprehend why the beautiful brunette with the gorgeous smile and endless curves wanted to spend time with someone like me. Stunned into silence, I stumbled out of the truck and watched her pull a bag of groceries from the backseat of her crossover SUV.

My foster mother's voice played through my head, snapping me out of the fucking stupor I'd fallen into. I could almost hear Mama Mae's voice chastising me for not offering to help Lily with her bags.

"Let me get that for you." I lifted the two bags out of her hands and led the way across the lot to the small cabin where I'd lived alone for the past three years. "Come on in. It's not much, but it's mine."

She entered through the front door and stepped into the two-story foyer. Her gaze swept over the thick log walls. "Did you build this place yourself?"

"I didn't start it, but I finished it." Working on the cabin had given me something to focus on besides trying to piece my broken life back together. "The foundation and walls were here, but I had to figure out the roof and build out the interior."

"It must have taken you a long time." Lily tilted her head back and looked up at the beams spanning the width of the structure.

Time was the one thing I'd had too much of back then. Working on the cabin wasn't traditional therapy, but spending every day in the summer sun kept me from feeling sorry for myself and wasting away. "The kitchen's right through here."

"Look, I even have a bottle of red wine." Lily stopped at the counter and pulled one thing after another out of the reusable grocery bags. "Do you have a corkscrew?"

I'd never felt as out of place as I did standing in my own kitchen. "Um, I don't know."

"If not, there's one on my keychain. It's in my purse by the door, if you don't mind grabbing it." She moved around my kitchen like she belonged there, pulling out pans and knives I'd forgotten I owned.

Feeling like an outsider, I moved toward the front door where she'd left her things. I grew up surrounded by brothers. I'd never lived with a woman before and didn't make a habit of going through their personal belongings. I grabbed her purse and carried it back into the kitchen with me.

Lily stood by the cutting board, dicing tomatoes into perfectly even chunks. "Should be right on top."

I peered into the bag. It felt like getting a glimpse of a foreign world. Thankfully, a set of keys caught my eye, and I pulled them out, grateful I hadn't needed to dig around.

"Good, you found them. Want to open the bottle so we can let it breathe?" She'd moved to the sink to fill a big pot with water.

I wasn't used to sharing my space. Wasn't used to following someone else's directions in my own kitchen, either. Yet, I reached for the bottle of wine and jabbed the corkscrew into the top. After I'd removed the cork, I opened the cabinet door and tried to find the closest thing I could to a wine glass. It was either coffee mugs or plastic juice glasses. Figuring it would be better to go with ceramic than plastic, I opted for the mugs.

After I poured us both a mug of wine, I settled onto a stool and watched Lily take control of my kitchen. She moved with the grace and confidence of someone who knew exactly what she was doing. Mesmerized, I took small sips of the wine and asked her to tell me what I could do to help.

"I've got everything under control. Just sit back and relax." She added pasta to the water she'd brought to a boil on the stove, then turned to stir something in a small pan.

"You don't know how weird it feels to have someone making me dinner in my own kitchen," I admitted. I'd never even had a woman over to my cabin before. The few visitors I'd had were all guys I knew from the Mustang Mountain Riders.

"Cooking helps me relax." She stopped moving long enough to pick up her coffee cup and hold it out to clink against mine. "I was pretty nervous before. Thanks for letting me make you dinner."

"You were nervous? About what?"

"About coming here. I could tell you were uncomfortable when you left the mercantile. Ruby encouraged me to go after you, but I didn't want to push you."

"I'm sorry. We hit it off so well the day we met at

the Easter egg hunt. I guess I didn't want your impression of me to be ruined."

Her brow creased. "Why would you think it would be ruined?"

I set down my wine and pulled myself up to my full height. "Look at me, Lily. I saw your reaction when you got a good glimpse of my face. Just once, I wish I could look at a beautiful woman like you without seeing the pity in her eyes."

"Is that how little you think of me?" Instead of her eyes softening with compassion, they narrowed. "You think I'm so caught up on a few scars that I can't see past them?"

I let out a dry laugh. "A few scars? Half of my face looks like a science experiment gone wrong. And you should see the rest of me."

She shook her head and lifted her hand toward my cheek. "The beauty I see in you goes way beyond skin deep."

I waited for her to pull back. Waited for her eyes to reflect the disgust and sympathy she must be feeling inside. Instead, her fingertips skimmed my right cheekbone. It had been years since I'd felt a woman's touch. I turned into it, stopping myself from nestling my cheek against her palm.

She was wrong. The sooner she realized it, the better off we'd both be.

Forcing myself to pull away, I stared down at her. "Any beauty you think you see is gone. It was burned away."

HE WAS SO STUBBORN, so strong-willed. Reminded me of one of the horses the guy next door had when I was a girl. The big stallion had been tied to a tree and left to starve. Our neighbor found it while he was hunting in the woods and brought it home with him. That horse had the same look in his eyes as Mack. The haunting look of a soul whose trust had been broken.

I reached forward again, tracing the contours of his face. The skin felt so different where he'd been burned. He thought it made him undesirable, but knowing what he'd been through had the opposite effect on me. Only a man with an inordinate amount of strength could have survived the ordeal he'd been through. Rising to my tiptoes, I gripped the front of his shirt with both of my hands and pulled him toward me.

He didn't resist, though I had the feeling I'd

pushed him just about as far as he was willing to go. At the risk of him pulling away, I pressed a feather-lite kiss to his cheek.

His chest expanded as he drew in a slow, deep breath. Neither of us moved. I couldn't tell if I'd ruined everything by being so bold.

Something in me sensed he'd needed to receive that kiss more than I needed to give it. I waited—each second that ticked by feeling like an hour.

A shrieking alarm pierced the silence. I immediately let go of his shirt and turned toward the stove where smoke billowed from the pan where I'd been sautéing some garlic in olive oil.

Mack charged toward the stove and grabbed the handle with an oven mitt. He tossed the pan into the sink and doused it with spray from the faucet. In a matter of a few seconds, the potential fire had been put out. Along with the heat that had ignited between us.

Mack turned off the faucet and put his hands on his hips. "That was close."

"I'm so sorry," I mumbled, my cheeks feeling like they were on fire themselves. "I guess I'm not much of a multitasker."

"Don't worry about it," he said. "Happens to the best of us."

He might be trying to make me feel better, but I could tell he was uncomfortable. His gaze darted away from mine as the lingering tension from our interrupted moment settled over the room.

"Maybe we should open a window," I suggested, attempting to regain some semblance of normalcy. "You know, air this place out a bit."

"Good idea." Mack moved to unlatch the nearest window. A gust of crisp mountain air flooded the room, carrying away the remnants of smoke and—hopefully— the remaining awkwardness between us.

"I can make something else," I suggested, trying to come up with a plan to salvage dinner as I rummaged through the rest of my groceries. "We've got the tomatoes I diced, plus I picked up some freshly grated Parmesan."

Mack rubbed the back of his neck. "Uh, sure, whatever you want to do."

"Great." I grabbed the container of Parmesan cheese and set it on the counter. As I pulled off the lid, I noticed Mack's hesitance. His gaze darted from the floor to the door, like he was searching for the quickest escape route.

"If you'd rather do something else, that would work, too." I didn't want to make him even more uncomfortable. "We could order pizza or something."

"No, it's not that." He glanced at the stovetop where the water still boiled. "It's just... I don't know. Can I be honest with you?"

"Of course." My pulse thundered through my veins while I waited for him to share his thoughts. Clearly, we were both out of our element.

"This whole thing is new to me. I haven't been on a

date in years. Not since my fiancé..." He glanced up, his eyes full of apology and pain.

My heart sank to the bottom of my belly. The moment we'd shared had been broken, and now the awkwardness was creeping in again like an uninvited guest. "I should go."

"Are you sure?" Mack asked, his expression a mixture of relief and disappointment.

"Yeah." I forced a smile. "I've got a lot to do tonight, anyway. I told Ruby I'd get her a suggested menu with pricing in the next couple of days. Thanks for letting me meet the dogs."

The mention of the dogs brought out a hint of a smile. "Thanks for being willing to make me dinner."

"At least let me clean up the mess I made." Not knowing what to do with my hands, I picked up the cutting board and knife and put them in the sink.

"I've got it." He stood by the edge of the counter like he couldn't wait to see me out.

It took all my willpower not to argue with him, but I figured he needed the solitude more than I needed to satisfy my urge to clean up after myself. "Okay, then."

He waited until I pulled on my jacket, then handed me the remaining groceries. "Thanks for stopping by."

As eager as he seemed to see the last of me, I hadn't gotten the confirmation Ruby needed. "What should I tell Ruby about the event?"

"Give me another day or two to think about it?"

His brows knit together like he wanted to say no but was too eager to send me on my way that he didn't want to take the time to explain himself.

"I'll let her know." I somehow made it down the steps and all the way to my car. As soon as I shoved the bag in the back seat and sat down behind the wheel, I sucked in a deep breath, trying to shake off the weight of what might have been.

I'd just pulled away from Mack's place when my phone rang. The display on the dash showed it was my assistant, Sam. I wasn't in the mood to talk to anyone, but we had a catering job the next day, so I needed to make sure she didn't have any questions.

"Hey, what's up?"

"I just stopped in at the mercantile and heard you were up at Mack's place this afternoon. Girlfriend, you need to tell me everything," she demanded. "Is he going to do the event with us? I don't know anyone who's ever been inside his cabin. What did it look like?"

"Slow down," I said, my voice cracking. "He said he needs some time to decide, but I think I might have ruined everything."

"How could you have done that? Unless... did he make a move on you? The two of you were awfully cozy at the Easter egg hunt, and I saw Ruby made him the mountain man of the month for May. Did you shut him down?"

Sam was a fabulous assistant, but had a tendency

to get carried away. "I don't want to talk about it right now. Let's just say I owe him an apology."

"You could make him some of those cookies we served at that corporate retreat we did last month. Remember? The ones with the caramel? People absolutely raved about them."

"I appreciate your enthusiasm, but maybe it's for the best. I mean, he moved all the way out there for a reason, right? Because he wanted to be alone. I'm sure he doesn't want me stopping by again, even if I have cookies with me."

"Or maybe he just needs someone to remind him that being around other people isn't so bad." Sam's voice took on a quiet, gentle edge. "I know Mack's stubborn, but so are you. And that's why Ruby probably thinks the two of you would work great together. It wouldn't hurt to make a good impression on Ruby Nelson, either. If you want to move the business to Bozeman, she's got connections there."

Sam was right. After several years in Whitefish, I was ready to expand and had applied for a small business loan that would enable me to move my catering business to a bigger town. As the mayor's wife, Ruby, had been to so many parties in Bozeman, she probably knew half the population. It would be in my best interest to stay on her good side.

I let out a groan, then caved and admitted it. "Fine. I'll make cookies and see if I can fix things with Mack. I hate it when you're right."

"Too bad it's more often than you want to admit."

Her smile came right through the phone. "I'll see you in the morning."

"Talk to you later." A renewed sense of determination flowed through my veins. I was going to prove to Mack—and myself—that we could overcome our awkward start to make Ruby's event a huge success.

THE AFTERNOON SUN hung low in the sky, casting long shadows across the grass. I climbed onto the four-wheeler, ready to take a few of my younger dogs on a quick run so we could practice the commands we'd been working on. With the mountains stretching up to touch the clouds, and the birds chattering to each other on the branches of the tall pines, I inhaled a deep breath of the crisp, fresh air. It was moments like these that made me feel alive and at peace, far away from my former life.

Tires crunched on the gravel as Lily's SUV pulled into the drive. My pulse jumped. It had been two days since she'd left. Two days of running through every moment we'd spent together to try to figure out how I could have handled things differently.

"Hey, Mack." Her voice carried over on the breeze. She gave me a slight wave with one hand while carefully balancing a plate wrapped in foil in the other.

The smell of something warm and sugary drifted through the air, making my stomach rumble.

"Hey." I climbed off the ATV and jogged over to meet her. The dogs weren't thrilled to have their run put on hold, and a few of them let me know with a couple of howls and yips. They could wait a few more minutes.

"Sorry to interrupt." She held the plate out to me. "I wanted to apologize for the other night, so I made you some cookies."

I took it from her while my gaze roamed over her face. Seeing her again made my chest squeeze tight. She was even prettier than I remembered. "Apologize for what? There's nothing you need to be sorry for, though I'll still gladly take your homemade cookies."

"I was out of line the other night." She toed at a rock wedged into the dirt. "And the cookies aren't a big deal. I was already doing some baking and thought you might enjoy them."

I didn't like the way she tried to downplay what she'd done. "It's not nothing. The last time somebody made me cookies was..." I tried to remember. "Hell, maybe never. Thank you. This means a lot."

A flush of pink swept up her cheeks. "In that case, you're welcome."

"I was just about to take a few of the younger dogs out on a dry training run." I glanced back to where I'd left the team harnessed to the four-wheeler. "Any chance you want to join me?"

"Really? That sounds like fun." Her face lit up like she was actually excited at the idea.

"Great." I knew she loved dogs by the way she handled them when she'd been here the other day, and getting her out on a run with me would be a great way to spend time together. I hadn't figured out where Lily might fit into my life, but I already knew I wanted her to be a part of it.

As I showed her how the harness was set up and introduced her to Triton and the dogs we'd be working with, I couldn't help but steal glances in her direction. Ever since she'd kissed me the other night, I felt like she'd touched a part of my heart that I'd locked away. I might not know exactly what I wanted to do about it, but for the first time since my accident, I felt the urge to see where things might lead.

"Okay, Lily, are you good to go?" I climbed on the four-wheeler in front of her, wishing we were on my Harley so she'd have to wrap her arms around me and hold on tight.

Her breath brushed the back of my neck. Goosebumps pebbled my skin. "Whenever you are."

"Ready," I told the dogs. They shifted into place and waited for me to give the final command that would send us on our way. "Alright!"

We took off down the path, with Triton setting the pace. The wind whipped past, and Lily's laughter bubbled up behind me. At that moment, it felt as if we had left our pasts behind and were racing towards something new, something filled with possibility, maybe even toward the beginning of building something between us.

"This is incredible," Lily yelled loud enough so I could hear her over the sound of the dogs' feet pounding on the hard earth.

"There's nothing quite like it." Exhilaration surged through my veins. Knowing she was enjoying something I loved made the experience extra sweet. "Back when I was a firefighter, I used to think that running into burning buildings would give me the biggest rush of adrenaline."

Her grip tightened, like she was encouraging me to go on.

"There's something about being here with these dogs, in this open space, that just sets me free." I couldn't keep the emotion out of my voice as I continued, "I guess it's because it feels like... hell, like I'm finally able to outrun my demons."

Lily rested her chin on my shoulder. "What happened to you back then?"

"Let's take a break." I gave the command for the dogs to stop and slowed the four-wheeler. I hadn't talked about the accident since I moved to Montana except to tell a few of the guys the obvious—that I'd been injured in a fire. The way Lily looked up at me, her eyes full of concern, told me I could trust her with my story.

"There was a house fire... a family was trapped inside. I knew the structure was about to collapse, but orders were to stand down until we'd been cleared to enter. Once we could go in, I did everything I could, but it was too late. A load-bearing beam came down, trapping me and the mom and kid inside."

"God, Mack, I'm so sorry." She reached out, gently resting her hand on my arm.

"I was lucky, but they didn't make it." I stared at her as I tried to shove the memories to the back of my mind. "It haunts me, Lily. Every fucking night, I see their faces in my dreams."

A shiver rolled through her, and I lifted my head to stare out across the landscape.

"I'd gladly trade places with them, but I can't. Being out here, surrounded by all of this beauty—it reminds me there's still some happiness left in this world."

"Like running with sled dogs and eating cookies?" She squeezed my arm.

"Exactly." Being with her and sharing a piece of my past made me feel lighter, like the heavy weight I carried around with me had eased just a bit. "Or like spending time with someone who bakes the best cookies in town and somehow manages to make everything better just by being around."

"Whoa," she teased, playfully nudging me with her elbow. "I think you might be overselling my cookie-baking skills. You haven't even tasted them yet."

"An oversight I plan on fixing as soon as we get back to the office." I gave her a shy grin, hoping I didn't scare her away again. "But I definitely mean the 'making everything better' part."

"So..." Her voice came out barely over a whisper. "I know it's not my place, but what you've been through is a lot. Have you talked to anyone about it?"

"Yeah," I funneled a hand through my hair, feeling slightly embarrassed. "The department made me talk to someone, but therapy didn't really do it for me. We kept going around in circles."

"Sometimes it's like that," she nodded, understanding in her eyes. "You have to find your own way to heal."

I nodded. "That's what brought me to Mustang Mountain. I started working with the sled dogs, and they've helped me more than I ever thought possible. There's something about them. Maybe their energy or the way they give it their all every time we head out on a run. They love what they do, and I guess it's contagious."

"Contagious, huh?" Lily smiled, looking at the pack of panting dogs around us. "They're amazing animals. I hope I can find something I love as much as they seem to love running. And look as good doing it."

"I'm pretty sure you'd look good doing just about anything," I joked, trying to keep things light.

"You wouldn't say that if you saw me the first time I tried to make fresh pasta." She laughed. "I probably still have flour in places you'd never expect."

I stopped myself from admitting I wouldn't mind looking for it. As we stood there in the golden hour, that time when the sun's rays made everything look more magical, I couldn't help but hope that Lily might be another piece of the puzzle on my path toward healing.

"Enough about me." I was never comfortable being the center of attention. "How's your catering business going? What made you decide to dive into that world?"

Lily glanced over, her eyes lighting up. "I've always loved spending time in the kitchen. I even used to pretend I had my own restaurant when I was a kid. My mom would place her order, and I'd serve her at the table."

"Really?" An image of a dark-haired, younger Lily floated through my mind. "I would have loved to see that."

"I've come a long way from serving mac and cheese from a box," she teased. "But I've always known I wanted to do something with food when I grew up. It's such an integral part of our lives, especially during celebrations. Sharing a meal brings people together and creates memories that can last forever."

Clearly, she was doing what she was meant to do. Her catering business seemed to be more of a calling than a job. It had been like that for me when I decided I wanted to become a firefighter. "That's a beautiful way to think about it."

"Thank you." A light pink stain flushed her cheeks.

She was gorgeous when she blushed. Damn, she was stunning all the time, but seeing that hint of vulnerability made me want to wrap my arms around her and hold on to her for the rest of my life. The rush of emotion threw me. I couldn't remember the last time I felt anything for anyone. I'd been numb for so long.

Lily continued. "As for the catering business, I saw a need not being served in the community, so I scraped together enough savings to get started, and here I am."

"I'm sure it wasn't as easy as that." Hearing her downplay the amount of effort it probably took to start her business didn't sit right with me.

"It wasn't." Her eyes narrowed like she was trying to figure out whether she wanted to let me in. "My dad bailed when I was a baby, and my mom and I didn't have much when I was growing up. She worked non-stop to put a roof over our heads and keep food on the table. Watching the sacrifices she made taught me I wanted to be in control of my own destiny."

"She sounds like a strong woman who loves you very much." I had no idea what it would feel like to have someone care that much about me. Besides Mama Mae, no one had ever made me feel worthy of love.

"She was." Lily swiped at her cheek.

The last thing I wanted to do was make her feel bad. I reached over and grabbed her hand. "I'm sorry. I didn't realize..."

Her fingers squeezed mine. "It's okay. How would you know? She's been gone a long time. Cancer sucks. I just wish she could see me now. When I think about everything she did for me... I'd love for her to know that I'm doing okay."

"You're doing more than okay. From what I've heard, you're doing great. And for what it's worth,"—I stopped and turned to face her—"I'm sure your mom's watching out for you. I'm sure she knows what an incredible woman you've become."

I could have kissed her then. Could have lowered my head and captured her full, pink lips with mine. I wanted to. Wanted it more than anything.

Triton barked, pulling us out of the moment. I wasn't sure whether I wanted to give him extra treats for saving me from making a potential mistake, or yell at him for ruining what might have been a moment that might change everything.

"I should probably get home." Lily squeezed my hand, then let it drop.

"Yeah, I need to get the dogs fed and settled in for the night. Should we head back?"

CHAPTER 6

LILY

I COULD HAVE TAKEN that opening to tell Mack about my plans to relocate my catering business to Bozeman. But until I heard back about whether my loan would be approved, there was no sense in talking about something that may or may not happen. Besides, he'd spooked so easily the other night. I didn't want to threaten the connection we were forging between us. There'd be plenty of time to fill him in later once I knew for sure what my future held.

Riding back to the office with the dogs leading the way, I tried to let go of my worries about tomorrow and enjoy the present: the wind whipping my hair around my face, the incredible view of the surrounding mountains, and the way my fingers dug into the solid mass of muscle sitting in front of me.

Too soon, we reached the start of the trail. Mack slowed the team and helped me off the back of the four-wheeler.

"I hope that wasn't too rough." He reached up to brush the hair out of my face, his gaze lingering on mine.

Nervous, I tried to swallow, but my mouth had gone completely dry. I cleared my throat and stared up at him. "Thanks for taking me. I had a really good time."

"We'll have to get you out on the trails when there's snow on the ground. Or maybe for one of the amateur race weekends. This is fun, but that's when the real magic happens." He looked down at me with new warmth in his eyes. It felt like a little bit of his protective shell had chipped away, revealing a glimpse of the man he used to be. The man he could be still if he'd let himself.

"I'd really like that." Anxious waves rippled through my belly. Assuming I was still around by then. I shook that thought away. Even if I did end up sticking around Mustang Mountain, I wouldn't be able to step away from my business for an entire weekend. Not if I wanted to keep it going.

"Thanks again for the cookies," Mack said. "I can't wait to try them."

"You'll have to let me know what you think." I pulled my keys out of my pocket. I'd done what I came to do: make peace and ensure I wasn't on Mack Webster's bad side. Being around him again made me realize how much I enjoyed his company. Before I could change my mind, I tossed out an invite to dinner.

"I suppose I owe you a make-up dinner since I didn't come through the other night."

"A make-up dinner, huh? I could probably get on board with that." There was a playfulness in his tone that hadn't been there before.

"I'm planning on testing the recipes I suggested to Ruby for the women's weekend event. I don't suppose you'd be interested in giving me your unbiased opinion, would you?"

"You're not going to smoke me out of my own kitchen again, are you?" His lips quirked up into a teasing smile.

I liked this side of him. Liked it more than I probably should. "You're never going to let me live that down, are you?"

"Your secret is safe with me." The smile faded, and I got the sense he was the type of man who could handle all of my secrets with room to spare. Not that I had any. "Doesn't mean I can't tease you about it though, right?"

I covered my face with my palms. "Ugh. Give me a chance to redeem myself, please?"

"You got it. I'll even bring the wine this time." He tugged my hands away from my face and wrapped his long, thick fingers around them. "And a corkscrew."

One of the dogs at the front of the team let out a howl. A few of the others joined in.

He let my hands go and turned toward the team. "I should get them settled."

"They really are incredible."

"Thanks. I don't know where I'd be without them. They've helped me through some pretty dark days. Especially Triton. He was the first and has probably taught me more over the years than I'd ever been able to teach him." Mack turned back to me and shrugged. "I guess you could say they threw me a lifeline."

"I'm glad you took it." I loved the look on his face when he talked about his dogs. The mutual respect they held for each other was obvious, even to a newbie like me. "I feel like my catering business has done the same for me. When my mom died, it was all I had."

He held my gaze for a few long beats. The connection between us strengthened, forged by the struggles we'd shared. Then he shifted his weight from one foot to the other, breaking the spell. "So when is this make-up dinner happening? I'll need to check my busy schedule to make sure I'm free."

"What are you doing Thursday night?" I didn't need to check my calendar. Except for my weekly Monday movie night with Sam, my nights were wide open.

"Gosh, I was going to see if I could play match-maker with Triton and Persephone, but I suppose it can wait." His wide smile told me he was teasing. "Figured I might give Ruby a run for her money if it works out and they fall in love."

"Do you think dogs are capable of falling in love?"

"That's an interesting question. I'll have to look into it and let you know." He gestured toward my SUV, sitting a dozen yards away. "Can I walk you to your car?"

"It's very chivalrous of you." I fell into step next to him, pausing when we reached the door while he opened it for me.

"I guess I'm a little bit old-fashioned when it comes to stuff like that." He waited until I got settled behind the wheel, then closed the door behind me.

I rolled down the window for a final goodbye, a little disappointed he hadn't tried to kiss me. It would make things so much easier if nothing happened between us, but I couldn't deny the attraction, at least on my end. "I'll see you Thursday. Seven o'clock work for you?"

"I'll be there." He lifted his hand to wave. "Hey, Lily?"

"Yes?"

"Thanks for telling me about your mom and how you got into catering. It means a lot that you felt comfortable sharing."

"Thanks for listening." Opening up had never been easy for me, but it felt right to share pieces of my past with Mack. My story was safe with him, just like the pain of his past would be safe with me. "I guess we've both found what we need in Mustang Mountain."

"Seems like it."

I backed up to turn around so I could head down the drive facing forward. A quick look in my rearview mirror showed him standing in front of the office with the dogs behind him. The sun reflected off the snow-peaked mountains in the distance, painting a picture I yearned to be a part of.

Then I turned onto the road that would take me down the mountain, already looking forward to Thursday night.

I SHIFTED my weight from one foot to the other while I stood on Lily's front porch and worked up the nerve to knock on the door. She lived in an older apartment complex halfway between Mustang Mountain and Whitefish. The idea of being so close to other people was enough to give me hives. Made me appreciate the privacy and space I had up at my cabin.

She'd invited me to dinner, but I wasn't sure if it counted as an official first date. It had only been a few days since she'd kissed me, but I wanted more.

I adjusted my grip on the bottle of red wine in my hand. Maybe I should have sprung for something more expensive. It wasn't like me to second guess myself, but I'd been doing a hell of a lot of that since Lily had entered my life.

I took a deep breath and knocked. A few moments dragged by until the door swung open.

Lily smiled up at me and the scent of something delicious made my mouth water. "You found me."

My chest squeezed at the sight of her. Tight jeans molded to her hips and her v-neck shirt clung to her curves and outlined the swell of her breasts. I wasn't prepared for the quick rush of blood that hurtled toward my cock.

"You okay, Mack?" Her brows arched, drawing my attention to her beautiful blue eyes.

Smooth, asshole, real smooth. Pulling myself together, I held out the bottle of wine and stated the obvious. "I said I'd bring wine. For dinner. Um, I mean, to drink with dinner."

Her eyes sparkled. "Thank you. I can't wait to try it. Do you want to come in?"

"Sure." I followed her into the foyer and closed the door behind me. Walking into her apartment felt like stepping into a hug from Lily herself.

A large, comfy couch took up most of the living room, and a flatscreen TV hung on the opposite wall. Two thick blankets draped over the back of a chair in the corner. One of them looked like it might have been handmade.

She set the bottle of wine down on the kitchen counter, then shoved her hands into two oven mitts. "Dinner should be ready in just a minute. Do you want to open up the wine?"

Nodding, I slid the travel corkscrew I'd bought when I picked up the wine out of my pocket. On the rare occasion I did have a drink, it was usually just a can of beer or a pour of whiskey. I'd never admit it to Lily, but I'd picked up a couple of spare bottles of wine to practice on last night just so I could make sure I didn't make a fool out of myself if she asked me to open the bottle.

"I hope you like pork chops." She pulled a dish from the oven and set it down on the counter.

"I'm easy. I pretty much like everything." The cork slid out of the bottle, and I let out a sigh of relief. At least that went well, though no doubt I'd have plenty of other opportunities to fuck something up before the end of the evening.

"I was going to serve the menu Ruby settled on for the event, but it didn't seem like enough." Lily bent down to reach into the oven again.

With her ass thrust up in the air like that, I forced myself to look away before I went full-chub. Beyond handling things by myself, I'd been celibate since my accident. Being around Lily was the worst kind of temptation, even though she had no idea what kind of effect she had on me.

"I'm sure it would have been fine. Anything's better than what I come up with on my own." I lifted the oven door to close it after she removed a tray of roasted vegetables.

Her lips curved into a smirk. "She decided to go with gourmet hot dogs to play off the sled dog demo."

"You're kidding me." Leave it to Ruby to cater in hot dogs. "If we had more time, I could get a couple of my brothers to head up here with one of their food trucks. They call it Hot Diggity Dogs and have even won a couple of awards."

"Well, doggone it. You never mentioned you have brothers." She scooped the roasted veggies into a bowl and handed it to me to carry over to the table.

"Foster brothers. I've got dozens of them."

Lily brought the platter of pork chops over. "Do they all live back in Texas?"

"We're spread all over, though I don't think any of them have moved to Montana except for me. Here, let me get that for you." I pulled her chair out from the table and sat down to her right. "Everything smells delicious."

"Dig in." She passed me the pork chops.

I slid one onto her plate before serving myself, my mouth already watering. I hadn't had a bite of food yet, but my mind had fast-forwarded ahead, wondering how the night would end. Would she be open to another kiss, or should we take things slow? As usual, I was overthinking things. We were just having dinner. She'd invited me over to try recipes she wanted to test out for Ruby's event.

But she wasn't serving me hot dogs. What did that mean? I hadn't been part of the dating world in almost a decade, though it felt like three times as long when I heard some of the stories the other guys shared.

"What do you think?" Lily cut a small bite from her pork chop, her gaze glued to her plate.

I wiped the corner of my mouth with the cloth napkin I'd set on my lap. "It's good. Really good."

Her lips curved into a slight smile. "I'm glad you like it."

My pulse evened out. There was no need to make tonight into something bigger than it was. We were friends. She'd seen some of my scars, and I'd told her about pieces of my past. If she hadn't run the other way yet, she wasn't going to judge me on how I held my fork or if I'd picked out the wrong kind of wine. I relaxed against the back of my chair.

Lily entertained me with tales from her early days in the kitchen. Apparently, burning garlic at my place was the most recent travesty in a long line of culinary disasters. We laughed while we worked our way through our meal and most of the bottle of wine. When I'd sopped up the last of the sauce on my plate with a fluffy yeast roll, I set my napkin on the table.

"I don't know how you can make food like that all the time and look as good as you do."

Her eyes widened like I'd just insulted her.

My gut clenched. "Hell, I'm sorry. I meant that as a compliment. Because you do. Look good, that is."

Fuck. I knew better than to make a comment like that. As soon as dinner was over, I was going to crawl back to my place and lock my lips together, so I didn't make an ass out of myself in front of her ever again.

She let out a soft laugh as she reached for her wine glass. "I hope you don't hate me for asking this, but are you nervous, Mack?"

"Is it that obvious?" I hung my head. "I'm so out of practice. It's pathetic."

"Should we move to the couch? It's probably more comfortable." Her chair scraped the hardwood floor as she pushed back from the table.

"Do you want me to help you clean up first?"

"I'll do the dishes later." She split the rest of the wine between our glasses and led the way to the living room.

I picked up my glass and followed, my heart thumping so loud that I was sure my buddies could hear it all the way up on the mountain.

"Sit down and tell me how long it's been since you've been on a date." She patted the cushion next to her as she kicked off her shoes and tucked her feet up underneath her.

"A first date?" I wracked the darkest recesses of my mind to come up with the answer. "It's got to be almost a decade. I haven't dated anyone since my accident, and I was with my fiancée for five years before that."

"You said something about being engaged the other night. I don't mean to pry, but did it not work out?" She leaned forward to set her wine glass down on the coffee table. "You know what? Scratch that. Prying is exactly what I'm doing, but you don't have to answer."

Her honesty made me chuckle. "It's okay. Turns out she didn't want to be with someone who wouldn't look good in the wedding pictures."

Lily's jaw dropped. "Nooooooo."

"Yeah." I waited for the familiar sting, but it didn't come. Either time had finally dulled the pain of that particular wound, or I'd gotten over the woman who'd broken my heart. Looking at Lily, I sensed it was the latter. "I suppose it was better to find out then that she wasn't the for-better-or-for-worse type than after we'd built a life together."

"There's got to be a special place in hell for people like that."

"You haven't seen the full extent of my damage." There it was. Not even my ex had seen all my scars. She'd bailed before I even left the hospital.

I didn't have a clue how Lily would respond to my comment, but climbing onto my lap and straddling my thighs sure as hell wasn't what I expected. Her fingers went to the top button of my shirt. "Show me?"

My chin lowered in agreement, and I closed my eyes while her fingers worked the button free. I was afraid to touch her, afraid to move. Her fingers skimmed over the scarred flesh between my neck and shoulder, followed by her lips.

"Is it getting hot in here?" I asked, angling my head to catch her lips in a kiss.

Her irises darkened to a deep navy blue. "I think it's just you."

"Is that right?" I skimmed my fingers under the hem of her shirt. Her skin was so soft, so perfect.

She sighed into my mouth, her hips rocking against mine. "I might be a little warm."

I deepened the kiss and moved my hands to her hair. She'd left it loose tonight, and I'd been imagining how it would feel to tangle it around my hands. It had been so long since I'd lost myself in a woman. Her scent was intoxicating, making me feel more drunk than if I'd downed another bottle of wine. I couldn't get enough of her.

She pulled back to trail kisses down the center of my chest, her fingers making quick work of my buttons.

I didn't want the moment to end, but it was inevitable. Once she saw me, the real me, there was no way she'd want to continue. So, I cupped her cheeks with my hands and pulled her mouth back to mine. The longer I could keep her attention on my mouth, the longer I could pretend.

KISSING MACK, I finally understood what all those girls back in high school had been talking about when they described what it felt like to have their breath stolen away. His lips teased and taunted, demanding more with each swipe of his tongue against mine. I breathed through my nose, desperate not to pull away until I had to.

The spicy scent of his cologne mixed with the earthy notes of the great outdoors. With my senses heightened, everything about him added to my growing need. The feel of his whiskers scraping along my jaw. The soft cotton of his shirt under my hands. The hardness of his erection bulging behind the zipper of his jeans.

I hadn't planned on sleeping with him when I invited him over for dinner, but this evening could only end one way. Unless I was willing to let my body spontaneously combust, I needed him. The hollow ache thrumming between my legs begged to be satisfied. I slipped his shirt over his shoulders and tugged the sleeves down his arms.

He tensed and pulled back, his eyes full of apprehension. My heart broke for what he'd been through. The man had suffered enough. I wanted him to know how beautiful he was, both inside and out.

"You don't have to—"

"Shh." I silenced him with a soft kiss, then gently pulled him to his feet. My gaze roamed over the puckered skin covering the right side of his body. In my mind, his scars were nothing more than a badge of courage—a sign of his strength.

He didn't move, didn't even breathe while I ran my fingers over each scar.

"You're perfect. Every single part of you," I whispered.

His fingers wrapped around my shoulders, and he crushed his mouth to mine. I held on, ready and willing to follow his lead.

"You could ruin me, Lily," he mumbled against my lips. "If I let you in, you could destroy me."

"No." I shook my head. "Just let me love you."

A strangled, desperate moan ripped free from his throat as he swept me up into his arms. He carried me down the hall and pushed my bedroom door open with his foot. We fell onto the bed together in a tangled mass of limbs.

In one fluid motion, he pulled my shirt up and over my head. His hands cupped my breasts, his thumbs grazing over my nipples through my bra. If his touch felt this good with my bra in the way, I couldn't begin to imagine how amazing it would be with nothing between us.

As if he could read my mind, he slipped a hand behind me and undid the clasp. I rubbed my thighs together, trying to alleviate the pulsing ache between them. It wouldn't take more than a brush of his fingertip over my clit to send me over the edge. As desperate as I was for his touch, I needed him to know how much I wanted him first, so I rolled us over so he was on his back. Then I ran my fingers over his chest, skimming the twisted, marred skin on his shoulder and tracing the ridges of scar tissue with my tongue.

When I came up for air, Mack lifted his head. "How can you do that?"

"How can I do what?" I rested my chin on his stomach, just inches above his waistband.

"Don't they disgust you?" Lines furrowed his brow.

I leaned forward, placing a soft kiss over his heart. Then I worked my way across his chest, kissing each scar, each angry line and twisted knot, showing him exactly what I thought of him.

"God, Lily. I've spent so much time trying to hide."

A tear slipped down my cheek at the heartbreak in his voice. "You don't have to hide anymore. I see you, all of you, and I've never wanted anyone more."

He rolled me over, his fingers moving to my waistband. I was more than willing to let him take what he needed, hoping it would be enough for him to start piecing himself back together again. His hands pushed my jeans down my legs, then he nestled his hips between my thighs.

I wrapped my legs around him, pulling him closer. His hand slid between us, gliding through my heat.

"I don't have anything with me. Sorry, I'll come prepared next time."

The thought of there being a next time made me bold. "Neither one of us has been with anyone else in a long time, and I'm on the pill."

"Are you sure?" He whispered against my ear.

I answered by spreading my legs. He shifted to pull down his pants, then kicked them off completely. Before they even landed on the floor, he nudged into me, his cock filling me slowly, inch by inch, until he'd seated himself deep inside. Then we moved together, our bodies in sync, finding a rhythm that transcended space and time.

My world fractured as I came undone around him. Huge waves of pleasure ripped through me, one right after the other, barely giving me a chance to catch my breath between them. I clung to his shoulders, my fingers digging deep into his skin.

"That's it, baby. I've got you." His words urged me on as another climax built within me. He joined me this time, thrusting deeper, moaning my name as he came. Spent, he collapsed on top of me, his arms supporting his weight.

I basked in the glow of the aftermath while tiny aftershocks pulsed deep within.

"It's too soon, and I'm probably ruining everything, but dammit, I love you, Lily." Mack rolled over, pulling me on top of him. His palm smoothed the hair away from my cheeks as he stared deep into my eyes. "Say something, sunshine."

I nuzzled into him and flung my leg over his hips. "Who cares if it's too soon? If it's what you feel, it's what you feel. I love you, too. All of you."

"How did I get so fucking lucky?" He lifted his head to capture my mouth in a kiss.

I corrected him. "I'm the lucky one. You just don't know me well enough yet to realize it."

"Doubtful. And for the record, I can't wait to get to know you that well." He adjusted his arm underneath me, pulling me even closer. "What are you doing for the rest of your life?"

My heart melted. "Maybe you should wait to see if I snore before you ask questions like that."

"Is that an invitation to spend the night?"

"Yes." I wanted to say it was an invitation to spend every night. In the short time we'd known each other, I could already tell he was capable of being my forever man. But something made me hesitate.

"I'll have to leave before you get up so I can go take care of the dogs." He pressed a kiss to my forehead. "Next time you should stay at my place."

"What makes you so sure there's going to be a next time?" I asked as I struggled to fight off sleep.

"Because when I give my heart, I give it forever. I'm not going anywhere, baby."

THERE'D BEEN a time when I thought no woman would ever be able to see past my scars, but Lily proved me wrong. The next two weeks passed in a blur, and I was happier than I'd been in a long damn time. Even my MC brothers commented on my new disposition, though I wasn't willing to admit the source. Caden figured it out, though. He came across Lily and me making out in the front seat of my truck one afternoon.

I'd sworn him to silence, but it wouldn't be long before word spread up and down the mountain and Ruby claimed another matchmaking victory. I didn't even give a fuck. Being in love with the kindest, most beautiful goddess in the world had that effect on me.

The sun filtered through the pines as I revved the engine of my Harley and waited for Lily to come down the stairs from her apartment. She'd wrapped up her prep work early, and I'd promised her an afternoon of exploring a few of the mountain roads, and hopefully, each other.

Her smile lit me up inside as she came down the steps. "You ready?"

"I'm always ready for you." I held the bike steady while she climbed on behind me, pulled on the helmet I handed her, and wrapped her arms around my waist.

Then we were off. I navigated the bike up the hills and into the base of the mountains. After an hour or so, I stopped by the hot springs. It had been almost eight hours since I'd tasted her, and I was almost at my limit.

"Come here, sunshine." I unfastened her helmet, eager to get my lips on her. "I missed you today."

She smiled against my mouth. "I missed you more."

We were turning into Jackson and Emma, or even worse, Ford and Luna. I'd made fun of them for not being able to keep their hands off each other, and now I was exactly the same.

"Are you hungry?" Lily slipped the straps of her backpack off and set the bag on the seat. "I brought you some of those caramel cookies you like."

"What do you call them again?" I took the one she handed me and bit into it. Ooooey, gooey caramel flooded my mouth.

"Caramel Cookies." Her nose scrunched up. She was fucking adorable. "Maybe I should come up with something better than that."

"I think you should call them Love Kisses."

"Look at you, showing your romantic side," she teased. "Why Love Kisses?"

I reached behind her and snagged another cookie, then broke it in two. Handing her half, I leaned forward and nudged my nose into her hair. Goose-bumps broke out over her arm. "Because these are the cookies that made me fall in love with you."

Her laugh echoed above the trees. "You make it sound like I baked some magic spell into them."

"Didn't you?" My arms circled her waist, and I pressed my hips against the curve of her belly. "I'm head over heels for you when I thought I'd never feel this way about anyone. If that's not magic..."

"It's not magic, it's love." She pulled back and stared straight into my eyes. "I think love is even more rare than magic, and I'm grateful I found it with you."

She had no idea how much she'd come to mean to me. I was willing to move mountains for her, or maybe even more. Maybe even face down my own demons so I could be the man she deserved.

"You know, I was thinking maybe we could do something for the volunteer firefighters in town."

"Oh, yeah?" Her eyes narrowed like she was trying to figure out what I was up to. "What do you have in mind?"

"Jonas said they're having a mandatory training tomorrow. Maybe we could take dinner over. Nothing fancy, just something to let them know they're appreci-ated." A lump lodged in my throat as her eyes softened around the edges. "The guys I used to work with never felt like cooking after a full day of training."

Lily nodded. "That's a great idea. Why don't we

stop by the store on the way home so we can pick up some supplies?"

I could have kissed her for not making a big deal out of my suggestion. After my accident, I'd never gone back to my old station before I moved away from Texas. It would have been too difficult to look those men in the eye, knowing I'd failed them. Even though the chief visited me every day while I was in the hospital and assured me I'd done everything in my power to save that family, I didn't believe him.

Over the past three years, I'd run through that night so many times in my head, I'd lost count. Though I was still heartbroken by the outcome, talking to Lily had made me realize the chief was right. It was time to start the long process of forgiving myself.

I spent the next morning as Lily's sous chef. She called out directions she thought I might be capable of following while she put together a four-course meal worthy of a five-star restaurant. I'd never seen her look sexier, especially when she slipped on a pink and black apron and tied a bow in the back. I shoved it in the bag when we left and made her promise she'd wear it for me later. Hopefully with nothing but a smile on underneath.

"Are you sure about this?" Lily squeezed my arm when we pulled up in front of the station. Worry lines furrowed the soft skin between her brows.

"Yeah,"—I rested my hand on hers and gave it a squeeze. "It's time."

The chief met us at the door and several of the

guys came out to help carry the food into the station. Seeing the way they interacted with each other—the easy banter they volleyed between them—took me back. Reminded me I hadn't always been such a loner. There'd been a time when I actually enjoyed being part of something bigger than myself.

Lily buzzed around, unwrapping the trays of made-from-scratch lasagna, tossing the dressing into the Caesar salad, and slicing the garlic bread. I tried to help, but she waved me off, so I followed the chief around and he introduced me to the few guys I didn't already know.

Jonas lifted his chin in acknowledgment from the far end of the table. He had a plate full of food sitting in front of him, but looked like he was almost too tired to eat.

"I sure don't miss days like this." Coming up behind him, I clapped him on the shoulder.

He grinned as he reached for his water bottle. "Can't say I blame you. They're killer. You doing okay?"

"More than okay." I glanced over to where Lily stood talking to one of the other volunteer firefighters.

"So, you and Lily?" Jonas asked.

"Yeah."

He nodded as he broke off a large chunk of garlic bread. "I'm happy for you."

"Thanks. Hey, don't miss out on the cookies. There's a whole tray of them over at the end of the table."

"What kind?" he asked around a bite of bread.

"Love Kissed. They're caramel and chocolate. Be careful though, they might just make you fall in love." Lily looked up and caught my eye. She shook her head slightly as she smiled and headed my way.

"Are you ready to go, or do you want to stick around a little bit longer?" Her arm went behind my back and she snuggled into my side. "I figured I'd stay at my place tonight since I'm meeting with Ruby and Courtney at the mercantile in the morning."

"Do you want me to come over after I check on the dogs?" I'd gotten used to falling asleep with her next to me and didn't like the prospect of spending even one night apart.

"You really have to ask?" She rose onto her tiptoes and gave me a quick peck on the cheek. A few of the guys hooted and hollered. I couldn't blame them. I would have done the same thing at the station back in Texas.

"Let's get out of here before you cause a riot." I wrapped my arm around her and led her outside. "You want me to follow you home before I head up the mountain?"

"No. The sooner you get your chores done, the sooner you'll come back to me." She sashayed toward her SUV and blew me a kiss when she reached the door. "If you hurry, you might even catch me in that apron you seem to like so much."

Nothing like giving a guy some incentive to hurry. I watched her pull out of the parking lot, then rushed over to my truck. It might be time to consider giving Caden even more responsibility. Or better yet, ask Lily to move in with me.

I PULLED into a spot in front of the mercantile, already running a few minutes late. Mack hadn't come over last night. He'd called to say Persephone had gotten out of her kennel and he and Caden spent half the night combing the side of the mountain looking for her. I'd stayed up until I heard she was safe, then told Mack to go to bed and get some sleep.

I'd gotten used to falling asleep in his arms, and I'd tossed and turned all night without him. Not even an extra cup of coffee this morning had been able to chase the sleepiness away.

The sun beat down on the front windows of the mercantile as I gathered my things to get out of the car. Ruby and Courtney were probably already waiting for me inside. I was in such a rush, I almost let the incoming call go to voicemail. Thinking it might be Mack, I grabbed for my phone and answered without checking the screen.

"Hello?"

"Miss Vandermere?" an unfamiliar, deep voice asked.

"Yes?" Assuming it was a telemarketer, I opened the driver's side door and got out of my SUV.

"This is a courtesy call from Wildwind Bank. Your loan for the Mountain Delight Catering Company has been approved. Would you like to set up a time to come in and sign the paperwork?"

My heart skipped a few beats. "I'm sorry, my what?"

He cleared his throat. "Your business loan. Looks like you applied several weeks ago."

A motorcycle rumbled past. I jerked my head up to see if it was Mack.

"Is this a bad time?" the man asked.

"No, um, this is fine. Sorry, I'm just walking into a meeting. Can I stop by later on this afternoon?" The bank was in Kalispell. I could head over after I finished up with Ruby and Courtney.

"How's two o'clock?"

"That would be great." It would even give me time to swing by the catering kitchen and check a few things off my to-do list before our meeting. Adrenaline buzzed through my veins. I'd been so distracted by everything happening with Mack, I'd lost track of how long it had been since I'd submitted my application. "Thank you so much for the call."

"We'll see you then."

The call ended, leaving me standing in front of the

mercantile with a dopey smile on my face. A dopey smile that lasted all of about five seconds when I realized what the call meant. My loan had been approved. The loan I'd been waiting on so I could move my business to Bozeman—almost five hours away.

My stomach rolled, and I grabbed hold of the light post to steady myself. Things between Mack and me were going so well. He'd shown me there was room in my life for both—my business and a boyfriend. A boyfriend that I hoped would turn into much more someday.

While my mind attempted to sort through the conflicting emotions swirling around inside, someone knocked on the front window of the mercantile. I glanced up to see Ruby motion for me to come in. There wasn't time to think about my relationship with Mack now. I shoved my concerns to the back of my head to deal with later and gulped down a huge breath of fresh air before entering the store.

"Are you okay this morning?" Ruby's eyes narrowed as she gave me a thorough once-over.

"Of course." With my luck, she'd start spreading rumors around town that I was losing my mind. I needed to perform some damage control, stat. "Is that a fresh pot of coffee I smell?"

Her eyes lit up with pride. "It sure is. I just made a new pot. Come on back. Courtney's probably ready for another cup. The two of us have been sitting here while we waited for you."

"I'm sorry I'm a few minutes late. I got caught on a

phone call about some last-minute details." I'd never admit the real reason for the call. Ruby would have a heyday if she caught wind of my plans. I needed to talk to Mack before anyone found out. If word got around before I had a chance to tell him myself... I didn't want to think about the fallout that might cause.

"Hey, Lily. Thanks for making yourself available this morning." Courtney gave me a smile as she flipped open a notebook on the table in front of her. I'd always liked her and had huge respect for the work she did at the women's shelter outside of town.

"Of course." I took the seat across from her. "When Ruby told me she wanted to donate a portion of the proceeds from the weekend to a local non-profit, I was excited to hear she'd chosen the shelter."

"We're lucky we receive so much support from everyone," Courtney said.

I gave Ruby a grateful smile as she set a cup of coffee in front of me. "Thanks, Ruby."

"My pleasure." She pulled up a chair and looked from me to Courtney and back again. "Now, how are we going to raise more money for the shelter from all of these women I'm bringing into town? I was thinking we could offer some local artists the opportunity to set up tables around the park kind of like a mini art fair. With a portion of their sales going to the shelter, of course."

"That's not a bad idea." Courtney lifted her mug to take a sip.

"I'd be happy to bake some extra cookies and

cupcakes we can sell if they'd like to take some home," I offered.

"And we could put together some baskets for a silent auction. I can offer a weekend stay in one of my rental cabins. Do you think Mack would donate a day-long sled dog trip?" Ruby turned to me.

"Um, I'm not sure. I can ask him." Right after I told him I might move five hours away, I thought to myself. It was hard to concentrate on my conversation with Ruby and Courtney with that hanging over my head.

"Great." Ruby rubbed her hands together. "I'll have Orville visit the shops downtown to see if any of them can donate a gift certificate or two. This is going to be so much fun."

Courtney bit back a grin. "It's more than I expected."

I knew exactly how she felt. "That's usually what happens when Ruby gets behind something."

"I've got another meeting to get to." Courtney slipped her jacket off the back of her chair. "Let me know if you need anything from me. It seems like there's still so much to do."

"You just keep doing the good work at the shelter, and leave the details to us," Ruby said.

While Courtney grabbed her things, my mind wandered to Mack. I wondered if he was still catching up on sleep from being up all night or if he might be thinking about me too. As much as I tried to convince myself he'd be supportive of me taking steps to grow my business, I couldn't help but worry that I'd have to let something go.

"So..." Ruby slapped her palm on the table. I jumped in response. "Tell me what's going on between you and my Mr. May. I know you've been avoiding me, but the cat's out of the bag now. Orville saw the two of you tighter than two peas in a pod at the feed store last week."

I groaned. "You have eyes everywhere, don't you?"

Her eyes twinkled. "What's wrong with wanting everyone to be as happy as Orville and me?"

Though her motives seemed pure, her methods could use some improvement. "I appreciate your interest in my love life, but it's getting a little complicated."

I hooked my finger through the handle of my mug and gave her a pointed stare.

"What do you mean? Orville said the two of you were in your own little bubble and didn't even notice him. Just like a pair of lovebirds." She let out a breathy sigh.

I had no intention of telling her I might move my business, but I also didn't want her to start ringing wedding bells. "It's just... everything is going really well with the catering business right now. I've finally reached a point where things are set to take off, and I don't want to lose my focus."

"Love does have a way of making a person rearrange their priorities. It's good to have ambition, but it won't keep you warm at night. Women today deserve to have both—the career and the man." Ruby nodded like she'd just solved all of my problems with a heaping helping of her age-old wisdom.

"People say that, but is it really possible?" I tried to ease my frustration by letting out a huge sigh. "I work seven days a week, sometimes twelve to fourteen-hour days. That doesn't leave much time for anything or anyone else."

Ruby set her hand on mine. "Us entrepreneurs have a hard time delegating, don't we? I almost turned Orville away, but then I took a long, hard look at what I wanted out of life and decided it was time to ask for help."

"Wait, you owned your own business when you and Orville met?"

"Sure did." She got up from the table to grab the carafe of coffee. "I grew up poor, honey. The kind of poor that leaves you with a hollow ache in your belly that never goes away. My folks did the best they could, but when there were bills to pay, mouths to feed, and not nearly enough money to go around, we just learned to do without. I started cleaning houses and babysitting to make my own money. By the time I entered high school, I'd moved onto sewing dresses for some of my friends."

I looked at her with fresh eyes. Maybe Ruby did have a pretty good understanding of where I was coming from.

"You've got options, hon, especially with Sam in your corner. Can't you let her take on more responsibility? You don't want to spend your whole life working your fingers to the bone, then turn around to realize you've run out of time to go after the things that really matter."

"Does it ever go away?" I asked. "That feeling that you'll never have enough?"

She pursed her lips like she was giving my question some serious consideration. "No. I still wake up some mornings in a panic, worried about a bill that's coming due or how I'm going to cover the inventory at the store. Going without for so long sticks with you forever, but you find ways to overcome it. Especially when you've got someone tall, dark, and handsome to tell you everything's going to be all right."

"Thanks. You've given me a lot to think about." If Ruby had been able to find a way to make things work, there wasn't any reason I couldn't do the same.

"Anytime, Lily. Now go home and give that mountain man of yours a big hug from me. And tell him he needs to give you something to smile about."

I laughed at the last bit, eager to do exactly that. Right after I stopped by the bank to figure out what to do about that loan.

MY PHONE RANG from where I'd left it on the counter. I was too irritated to talk to anyone. Unless it was Lily calling, I planned to ignore it. Squinting at the caller ID, I could barely make out my buddy's name. Jonas.

"Do you want to get that?" Caden asked. He'd been walking around on eggshells since he woke me up to tell me Persephone had gotten out again. After chasing her all over the mountain last night, I was tempted to let her go. That feeling only lasted a few seconds before I dragged my tired ass out of bed and tracked her down on the four-wheeler.

"He'll call back if it's important." I stared at the hole in the side of her kennel. "Hades had to have done this. None of the dogs were loose, and he's been trying to get close to her ever since she went into heat."

The phone rang again. Dammit. Whatever Jonas wanted, it couldn't be good. His twin Jensen ran point as the club's main contact for the women's shelter. Maybe they needed a few of the guys to help out with a domestic situation. Figuring that must be the case, I reached for the phone. "Hey, what's up?"

"Is it true? Is Lily moving her catering business to Bozeman?" Jonas asked.

"What the fuck are you talking about? Where did you hear that?" There had to be a mistake or some kind of misunderstanding.

"I just had a text from one of my exes who works at a bank over in Kalispell. Lily came in today to sign a bunch of papers for some loan. Said she'd applied, so she'd have money to move to Bozeman and expand." Jonas paused like he was waiting for me to say something. "Did you know she'd applied for a loan?"

"I've gotta go." I hung up without saying goodbye. Lily was leaving. The realization slammed into me like a sucker punch to the gut. I gritted my teeth against the surge of emotions threatening to suck me under.

I'd been a fucking idiot to think she'd be happy with me. She was beautiful. And I was... hell... I buried my head in my hands... I was a monster.

I needed to see her, needed her to tell me in her own words why she'd led me on.

"I'll be back in a little bit," I told Caden. "Try not to lose another dog while I'm gone?"

He didn't deserve the brunt of my anger, but at the moment, I didn't care. The only thing I could think about was Lily leaving. Even after all the time we'd spent together, all the secrets we'd shared. I felt like she'd opened me up and filleted me like a fucking fish. I felt gutted.

Her SUV sat in front of her apartment building in its usual spot. My hands shook as I got out of my truck. A part of my brain argued that it might make sense to take some time to cool down before I confronted her. I didn't know the whole story. Jonas's friend might have gotten the facts mixed up.

Then she opened the door and stepped out onto the stoop. The late afternoon light brought out the highlights in her dark hair. Even now, with my heart shattering into a billion pieces, I still loved her.

Her eyes lit up when she saw me. "Hey, Mack. What are you doing here? I tried to call you a little bit ago, but you didn't answer."

I ran my hand over my pocket. Dammit. I'd left my phone back at the office. "I got a call from one of my MC brothers. Said a friend of his saw you signing some papers over in Kalispell this afternoon. Is there something you want to tell me, sunshine?"

She drew in a wobbly breath. "Do you want to come inside? We need to talk."

I couldn't bear to hear the news in her apartment. Not when the last time I'd been there, I thought she was mine. "I'd rather talk right here."

She reached for my hand. I let her take it but didn't react. "It's true. Several weeks ago, I applied for a loan. I'm running out of space at the location in town. I wanted to use the money to expand."

"Why didn't you tell me you planned on leaving?" I

asked. "You never said anything about expanding your business. I thought you were happy here, Lily. Happy with me."

"I was." She shook her head. "I mean, I am."

Looking at her hurt too much. I lifted my head and stared at the bright blue sky overhead, hoping it might provide me with the answers I needed. "Were you ever going to tell me, or were you just going to disappear? Maybe send a card at the holidays?"

"That's not fair." Lily tightened her grip on my hand. "It's not like that."

"What's it like then?" I ground out. I was being an ass, but I was powerless to stop myself. Desperate to pull my hand from hers, I couldn't. Even now, I craved her touch.

"I've worked my ass off to make sure I never end up in the same position as my mom did. You can't expect me to give all of that up because we fell in love. It's not that easy." Her eyes begged for me to understand.

"That's where you're wrong. Falling in love shouldn't make you feel like you have to give something up. It should make you feel like you're gaining some-thing. Or maybe not something, but someone. Someone you can lean on. Someone you can trust to be there for you, no matter what." I waited for her to say something. Anything.

When she didn't, I closed my eyes and finally pulled my hand from her grip.

"Mack?" she whispered. "Let's talk about this. It doesn't have to be the end."

I swallowed hard against the lump in my throat and steeled myself for what needed to be done to protect what little remained of my heart. When I opened my eyes, I looked past her, refusing to meet her gaze. "I think we've both said what we needed to say."

Then I turned and walked back to my truck, each step carrying me farther away from her. Farther from a future I'd been naïve enough to believe in.

IT HAD BEEN over a month since Ruby's women's weekend. I'd hoped Mack and I could work things out, but he hadn't even bothered to show up that day and had sent Caden to do the sled dog demo instead. At least we'd raised a few thousand dollars for the shelter.

That's when I knew it was really over. A week later, Sam and I had packed up the catering business and moved to Bozeman. Getting settled in our new location had kept me so busy I hadn't had a chance to catch my breath. I was grateful for the distraction. If I stood still for too long, the pain would catch up and overtake me. Leaving Mack had been the hardest thing I'd ever had to do.

Even now, I second-guessed my decision. Then I'd get a new order or set up a meeting with a prospective client, and I'd push those feelings down, hoping they wouldn't surface again. Maybe Ruby could have it all, but that didn't seem to be in the cards for me.

After the ribbon cutting this afternoon, I'd feel better about things. That's what I kept telling myself. I hoped with all my heart—or at least what was left of it —that it would be true.

"You'll never guess who's here." Sam came through the double doors into the commercial kitchen. "Not only did the president of the local chamber show, but the mayor and his mother are eager to meet you."

"The mayor?" I'd posted an announcement in the events section of the local paper about our ribbon cutting, but I didn't expect the mayor to stop by.

"His mom's a doll. Says she's a friend of Ruby's from way back. I told you Ruby has connections all over the state." Sam beamed, and I summoned a smile in return. Too bad her enthusiasm wasn't contagious. I could use a double shot of that right about now.

"How do I look?" My voice cracked as I smoothed my palms over the apron I'd pulled on over my shirt. It reminded me of Mack, of that night we'd joked about him coming over to find me in nothing but an apron and a smile.

"Are you sure you're okay?" Sam asked. Her smile faded, replaced with a look of concern.

"I'm fine." Nodding, I linked my arm through hers. "Let's go cut the ribbon and meet the mayor. Maybe his mom can tell us some stories about Ruby."

THE GRAND OPENING open house was a success. One of the local news stations showed up and asked if

I'd be interested in being featured in one of their small business profiles next month. The mayor's mom was even more fun than Sam anticipated. She told us how she and Ruby used to skip high school to go spy on the mountain men who worked at the lumber mill. All in all, it was a successful event. But when it was over and we'd put the last serving platter away, I still felt empty.

I loved our new location, had a calendar full of bookings, and had hired some amazing staff who were excited to help me build up the business.

But I missed Mustang Mountain.

Even more than that, I missed Mack.

I hadn't heard from him since I left, and knowing him as well as I thought I did, I didn't expect him to reach out.

"Hey, do you mind if I take off?" Sam untied her apron and hung it on a hook by the back door. "A few of our new hires asked if I wanted to meet up after. I guess there's a place that plays live music on Thursday nights."

"Yeah, there's not much left to do. I'll finish up here." I gave her a tight smile. No use dwelling on thinking about what might have been, not when the future I'd dreamed about was unfolding right in front of me.

"Do you want to come with us?" Sam asked. Being in Bozeman might be dragging me down, but it had the opposite effect on her. There was a bounce in her step that hadn't been there before. She'd always had a positive attitude, but since she'd left Mustang Mountain, she positively glowed.

"No. I'm worn out. My afternoon and evening are going to involve a glass of red wine and a long, warm bath."

She studied me for a long beat. Then she shook her head. "It might not be my place, but someone needs to tell you the truth."

The blood rushed from my cheeks. "The truth about what?"

"Look at you. It's been over a month. Moving the business might have been your dream, but you're miserable."

"I am not." Even as I said the words, I knew she was right. I was just too stubborn to admit it to anyone, especially myself.

Sam put her hands on her hips and stared me down. "I've heard you crying in the bathroom."

"Okay, so I'm a little sad. It will pass. Time heals all wounds. Isn't that what they say?"

Her expression softened, and she reached out to put a hand on my arm. "Maybe 'they' aren't in love with Mack Webster."

"It's not that easy." I shook off her hand and paced across the kitchen floor while thoughts of Mack swirled around in my head. "I've been working at this business for years. All the plans I made and the dreams I had, they're finally happening."

"Dreams can change." Her shoulders shrugged.

"What am I supposed to do? Knock on his front

door and say I changed my mind? That I thought I could move on without him? That I made a mistake?" I searched her face for answers.

"Well, yeah."

"What happens next? My life is here. He belongs there." There was no way it could work. Mack would never leave Mustang Mountain. It was his refuge, the one place where he could be himself, where he felt free.

"What happens next is up to the two of you. You've got options. He can move here, or you can hire a capable, amazing manager to handle the day-to-day stuff in Bozeman and work from Mustang Mountain a few days a week." She looked at me like she was explaining how to get the answer to something as simple as adding two plus two.

A sliver of hope wedged its way into my chest. Would it really be that easy? Then an image of Mack's face filled my mind. That last day I saw him... he'd been so angry. No, not angry. He'd been hurt, and I'd been the one who'd hurt him. What I'd done to him was worse than his fiancé leaving him at the hospital. I'd built him back up, showed him I loved him for who he was, scars and all.

Then I'd abandoned him.

Tears filled my eyes. "He'll never be able to forgive me."

"Maybe he won't," Sam said, her lips drawn into a tight line. "But wouldn't you rather know for sure than always wonder?"

I swallowed the prickly lump in the back of my throat. "Yeah. I think I would."

Sam pulled her apron off the hook and re-tied it behind her back.

"What are you doing?"

"Someone's got to manage things over the next few days while you head back to Mustang Mountain."

I held out my arms and wrapped her in a huge hug. "I'm so lucky to have a friend like you."

She wasn't the type to get emotional, but I could have sworn I saw the glimmer of a tear in the corner of her eye.

"Let's go over the events we have for the next two days. If we hurry, you ought to be on the road in less than an hour and might even catch him before he turns in for the night."

THE ROAR of my motorcycle ricocheted off the brick walls of the buildings in the alley behind the Mountain Delight Catering Company. My ass ached from the five-hour ride, a small price to pay for the chance to see Lily again. Ruby told me about the grand opening celebration two weeks ago. I'd gone back and forth, trying to decide if I had the balls to show up.

In the end, my heart made the call. I couldn't stay away. But now, looking at the curvy script of the small sign hanging on her back door, my heart pounded in my chest, a mixture of nerves and anticipation churning in my gut.

I hadn't been able to stop thinking about her. The way her eyes lit up when she talked about an event she'd just booked, the feel of her thighs aligned with mine as we drove over the back mountain roads together, and especially the way it felt to wake up with her in my arms. I finally pulled my head out of my own ass and decided I didn't want to live another day without that.

Without her.

Steeling my nerves, I lifted a hand and knocked on the back door. I'd missed the party, but the lights burning inside let me know someone was still there. Probably Lily prepping for a job the next day.

The door creaked open, and my heart stalled. Sam stared out at me. "Mack?"

"Yeah. Sorry, I tried the front door, but it was locked."

"What are you doing here?" The scent of fresh-baked bread and something sweeter drifted out to tease my nose.

"I came to see Lily. Is she around?"

"Um, yeah. She was just getting ready to—"

"To come see you." Lily filled the doorway next to Sam. She was still all dressed up from hosting the ribbon cutting.

The urge to pull her into my arms washed over me. I flexed my fingers, biding my time. If all went well, I'd be burying my nose in her hair and pressing against her curves in the immediate future.

"What do you mean?" My gaze ran over her face. Her perfect nose. Eyes the color of a brilliant Montana summer sky. The full lips I hadn't been able to stop dreaming about.

"Sheesh. Haven't either of you heard of texting? Imagine if you missed each other. You could be driving back and forth for days." Sam shook her head and stepped through the doorway. "I was just leaving. See you tomorrow, Lily."

Lily lifted her hand in a distracted wave, her eyes never straying from mine. "What are you doing here?"

"Can I come in?" I was prepared to deliver my message anywhere, but standing in the alley with a dumpster full of Indian food from the restaurant next door wasn't exactly romantic.

She moved away from the door and further into the kitchen. The tightness in my chest eased a fraction. As I stepped into the light, I glanced around her new space. Brand new stainless steel counters sparkled. She'd doubled the room she had back in Mustang Mountain. I was proud of her. She'd gone after her dreams and hadn't let anything or anyone stand in her way. Not even me.

"What are you doing here?" Her voice tugged at my attention.

"I needed to tell you something. Were you really about to head back to Mustang Mountain?"

She tilted her head, her expression growing even softer. "I needed to tell you something too."

"Ladies first." I stopped trying to hold back my smile and let it break free.

Her lips curved up, matching my grin. "Always the perfect gentleman."

I bit down on my lip and shrugged while I waited for her to continue.

"I miss you, Mack." Her voice filled with emotion. "Leaving you was a mistake. I know that now. I should have been upfront with you so we could figure out a plan together."

Hearing her say that, knowing the pain I felt when she left hadn't been one-sided, I had to agree. "Loving someone means you don't have to do things on your own. But loving someone also means letting them go when you think that's what will make them happy. That's what I tried to do for you. Tried and failed since I'm standing here now, asking for another chance."

She blinked a few times as she took a step closer. "You want another chance?"

I was done fighting the need to touch her. I reached out and tucked a few strands of hair behind her ear, caressing her cheek as I told her the truth. "You're my light. I'm fucking lost without you, sunshine."

Her face crumpled as she flung herself at me. I caught her, cupped my hands under her ass and lifted her up so I could capture her mouth in a searing kiss.

She wrapped her legs around my waist, clasping them behind my back. "I'm lost without you, too. That's what I was coming to tell you. I don't want to be without you. There's got to be some way we can make it work."

"You up for going for a little ride?" I mumbled against the sweet, soft skin of her cheek.

"On the bike?"

"Yeah, baby. On the bike. There's something I want to show you."

. . .

TWENTY MINUTES LATER, I stopped at the edge of a clearing. A cozy cabin sat in the center of a large plot of acreage. I'd been scoping out properties online for a few days, and had driven by this place on my way into town. It wasn't Mustang Mountain, but it was close to Lily and that's the only thing that mattered.

"What's this?" Her thighs squeezed mine.

"That depends on you." I got off the bike and held out a hand to help her. "I figured the kennels could go over there by the trees, and that leaves plenty of room to add onto the cabin. It's small on the inside, but we don't need much room since I don't plan on ever leaving your side."

"You want to move your business to Bozeman?" Her forehead wrinkled as she worked through what that might look like for us. "You're willing to do that for me?"

I turned to face her, clasping my hands together above the swell of her ass. "I'd do anything for you. As long as we can be together."

"But Mustang Mountain is your home."

She still didn't get it. "You're my home, sunshine. Yeah, I love my place on the mountain, but none of it means a damn thing unless you're there to share it with me."

"That's not going to work." In a matter of seconds, she'd splintered the hope that had been building up in my chest. "You belong in Mustang Mountain."

I shook my head, not willing to let her go this time.

"And I belong with you," she finished.

"I won't let you give up your dreams for me."

"I'm not. A good friend recently told me that dreams can change. I got so focused on sticking to my plan, I lost sight of that. There's no happy ever after for me without you in it." Her hands went to my cheeks.

I could see the truth in her eyes. Cupping her face in my hands, I wiped a stray tear from the corner of her eye. "I want to spend the rest of my life with you, no matter where we are."

"That's what I want, too."

My heart swelled as I pulled her close, slanting my mouth over hers in a kiss full of promises I intended to keep.

When she finally pulled back, I reached into my pocket and slid a collar into her hands. "There's one more thing. If we're going to be together, you're going to have to have your own sled dog team. I'm giving you Persephone. She's ready to become a lead, at least after she weans the litter of pups she's expecting."

"We're expecting puppies?" Lily took the collar and threw her arms around me again, almost knocking me flat on my ass.

"Yeah. Hades got to her. I sure hope the puppies take after their mom. Though he's definitely been showing a softer side since he's been hanging around looking after her."

"I can't wait to see them." She rose to her tiptoes and pressed a sweet kiss to my lips. "What do you think about me making Sam a partner in the business?

She can stay in Bozeman and manage this location while I come back to Mustang Mountain with you and re-open the original Mountain Delight Catering Company?"

My grip around her waist tightened. "I think that would make me the happiest man in the world." I held her tight, breathing her in, my heart overflowing with possibilities for the future we could build.

We had a long road ahead of us, but if we traveled it together, we'd be able to tackle any roadblocks life might put in our way.

After all, we'd already overcome the biggest challenge of all. We'd realized we were stronger together than we'd ever be apart. We'd found our way back to each other.

EPILOGUE

JENSEN

I NORMALLY ENJOY Sunday night dinners at Aunt Ruby's house. She's a damn good cook and besides my twin brother Jonas, she and Uncle Orville are the closest family I have. Usually, there's good food and dessert, even if we have to deal with a little bit of Aunt Ruby's gossip and some talk about how we need to find nice girls.

That talk has been coming up more and more as my MC brothers have been finding love, and Aunt Ruby is really laying it on thick tonight. The reason she's harping on us to find nice girls and settle down becomes painfully clear when I get a text from Luna.

> Luna: Have you seen this?

That's all her text says, but there's a link to the Mustang Mountain tourism website that my aunt runs, and I get a sinking feeling in my stomach as I click the link.

Jonas and I went to school with Jackson, Ford, and Luna. We were a grade behind Ford and Luna, so it wasn't really until we became adults that we all reconnected, but they've become a second family to us. So I know for her to reach out it must be big.

When the page loads, I jump out of my seat, and in a few long strides, I'm in the kitchen where my aunt is cleaning up dishes from dinner.

"What the hell is this, Aunt Ruby?" I ask, showing her the page where she has me listed as Mustang Mountain's Mountain Man of the Month for June.

"Boy, you better watch your mouth! Adult or not, I'll still pop you upside the head with a frozen steak if you cuss like that in my house again." Aunt Ruby turns around to glare at me. Then she glances at the website and shrugs her shoulders. "It's about time you and your brother settle down if you expect me to be any kind of grandparent figure to any kids you might have. You'd better get going. Your Uncle Orville and I aren't getting any younger."

Jonas walks into the kitchen laughing hysterically. "I knew you were going to be June. I just knew it."

"You'd better shut your mouth because your name starts with a J, and I'd bet anything that she's got you set up to be July." That seems to sober him up pretty quickly as he looks over at Aunt Ruby.

"She wouldn't dare," he says, as if Aunt Ruby isn't standing in the room.

"I would dare. Now get your butt in gear and help me with these dishes," she says, handing the sponge in her hand to Jonas just as my phone starts to ring.

Aunt Ruby glares at me, but I hold up my phone. "It's Courtney," is all I have to say, and Aunt Ruby nods.

She approves of Courtney and me working together to help the women's shelter. I've been the main point of contact when Courtney needs help from my MC brothers, so I get random calls from her at odd times.

"Hey, Courtney," I say as I answer the phone.

"Hey, Jensen, I need your help. I've got a woman who called, and she and her daughter need to get out of a very unsafe situation tonight. I need backup."

"You've got it. I'll meet you at the normal spot?"

"I'm already on my way there. The sooner you can get there, the better. This one's not pretty," she says, and my blood goes cold. Generally, when Courtney says something like that, it means there are kids involved.

Some of the situations Courtney has helped women out of are things straight out of your worst nightmare's nightmare. Things your brain can't comprehend.

We don't even bother saying goodbye, we just hang up. Every second counts.

"Jonas, we've got to go now. Courtney needs our help with a really bad case," I tell him, and he drops what he's doing.

"Damn it, we have the bikes," he says, talking about our motorcycles, which will make it impossible to make phone calls to the rest of the guys on the way.

"Who do you need me to call?" Aunt Ruby asks.

"Ace and Shaw. Let's let the married guys have a peaceful night on this one," I tell her. She nods, already pulling out her phone.

We each give her a kiss on the cheek and then rush out the door.

Our meeting spot is at the base of the mountain. Ace and Shaw beat us there by a minute or two. I can see the tension on Courtney's face.

We don't waste time with hellos. She just nods, and we follow her down the road. She's in the women's shelters pick-up, a vehicle I insisted on when I found out she was doing pickups in her personal car.

I made an issue about how unsafe it was for people to know her vehicle around town, so now she has a vehicle specifically for these types of pickups at the women's shelter.

The four of us ride behind her on our bikes. Now that the weather is warm, we're going to get them out as much as we can. Plus, they make for pretty quick getaway vehicles if we need to provide a distraction for her, which we've had to do many times.

All my brothers in the MC club know exactly what to do. We've all helped on these runs. Honestly, it's part of what built our MC club to begin with.

We arrive at an old, rundown house that doesn't look like it would be habitable for a human being. The only sign of life is a child's tricycle overturned on the overgrown grass in front of the house.

The place is closer to Whitefish than Mustang Mountain, but we've traveled several hours to help someone in need before, so distance doesn't matter.

No sooner do I turn off my bike and get off to walk up with Courtney than a woman steps out of the house. The other men stay on their bikes in case they need to use them to help protect Courtney and me, or block someone from entering or leaving the house.

"Hurry, he's going to be back anytime now. He just got out of work early." Her frightened voice tells me she wasn't expecting the man back so soon.

As she steps into the yard, I can see the woman has a toddler on her hip. Thankfully, the vehicle Courtney uses has car seats in it. Courtney helps the woman get her daughter secured as I grabbed the bags sitting by the front door.

As expected, there are only three bags. These women usually leave with very little. Some of them don't even get out with anything at all.

I grab all three bags and toss them in the back of the truck Courtney's driving.

"Alright, let's go," Courtney says as the woman gets into the car. We waste no time getting Courtney back down the road and making sure she's not followed.

We don't pass another car until we get to the main road and head back towards Mustang Mountain. My job is to stay with Courtney if she needs anything. The other guys are making sure that we're not followed.

Thankfully, tonight seems to be a pretty easy ride as we get back to the spot where we met up with Courtney earlier tonight.

This is where we part ways with the guys. We don't want to overwhelm the woman, who more than likely would be terrified of four hulking tattooed bikers surrounding her. Not to mention that the rest of the guys have never been to the women's shelter. We keep the location under lock and key, so it's not easy to find on top of all the security measures I've made sure they have in place.

I'm the only guy from the Mustang Mountain Riders that has actually been to the shelter outside of my brother Jonas. Once the other guys are gone, I follow Courtney the rest of the way to the shelter. There's a locked gate at the road as we turn onto the driveway. The whole area is fenced in with security measures that I've set up, including cameras.

It's a mile-long driveway, so even if there was no gate, someone still wouldn't be able to see the place from the road. Plus, the land backs up to a mountain, so it's pretty secure.

Once Courtney parks the vehicle, one of the other women that works at the intake part of the shelter steps out, and Courtney takes a few minutes to explain the process to the woman while I stand back. The woman hesitantly steps out, then looks over at me and gives me a shy, shaky smile.

It's then I get a good look at her and the bruises that cover her body. She has a black eye, a split lip, and blood at the hairline near her temple. Distinct bruises in the shape of handprints fill her arm that's holding her daughter, and her daughter has a fresh bruise on her arm as well.

Her little girl looks to be in much better shape than she is, and my guess is her last straw was when the guy put his hands on her daughter. Usually, the women are more than fine taking the beatings themselves, but when their kids are brought into the mix, that's where they draw the line. I hate that it has to get that far before they'll call for help, but I'm glad they call, regardless.

Once the woman is safely inside, Courtney turns back to me. I get off the bike, set my helmet on the handlebars, and walk over to her before pulling her into my arms.

"Thank you for tonight," she says.

I know Courtney will sit out here for a few minutes and process what happened before she goes inside. She also knows that I won't leave until she is safely inside because I know she'll be spending the night here.

"I'm here anytime you need me, Courtney. You know that," I tell her, holding her a bit tighter.

It's moments like this that make me wonder why Jonas ever broke up with her. I hate that they dated in high school in the first place, making her off-limits to me.

"I know, but I still really appreciate it. I'm going to need a day or two to make sure she gets settled in, but we still need to get together to talk about the outing we have planned for the women and kids here."

There's a medieval festival a few towns over and she really wants to take the women and children out for the day to let the kids relax and just be kids. But for the women to feel safe enough to go, they'll need support, and they'll need protection.

That means all the Mustang Mountain Riders will be there, even the elders. The club voted to make this outing one of the mandatory events all the guys need to attend. It's not like we could put up a signup form asking for volunteers without drawing attention to the women's shelter and the people we've been protecting.

I'll take any time I can with her, because even if she's off limits, it hasn't stopped me from wanting her.

Want to read more about Mack and Lily? Get a free bonus scene here: https://www.matchofthemonth books.com/Mack-Bonus

Get the next two books in the series now... Jensen and Jonas Pike who just happen to be twins:

June is for Jensen - https://www.matchofthemonth books.com/June-Jensen

July is for Jonas - https://www.matchofthemonth books.com/July-Jonas

MOUNTAIN MEN OF MUSTANG MOUNTAIN

Welcome to Mustang Mountain where love runs as wild as the free-spirited horses who roam the hillsides. Framed by rivers, lakes, and breathtaking mountains, it's also the place the Mountain Men of Mustang Mountain call home. They might be rugged and reclusive, but they'll risk their hearts for the curvy girls they love.

To learn more about the Mountain Men of Mustang Mountain, visit our website (https://www.matchofthe monthbooks.com/) join our newsletter here (http:// subscribepage.io/MatchOfTheMonth) or follow our Patreon here (https://www.patreon.com/MatchOfThe Month)

January is for Jackson - https://www.matchofthe monthbooks.com/January-Jackson

February is for Ford - https://www.matchofthe
monthbooks.com/February-Ford

March is for Miles - https://www.matchofthemon
thbooks.com/March-Miles

April is for Asher - https://www.matchofthemonth
books.com/April-Asher

May is for Mack - https://www.matchofthemonth
books.com/May-Mack

June is for Jensen - https://www.matchofthemonth
books.com/June-Jensen

July is for Jonas - https://www.matchofthemonth
books.com/July-Jonas

ACKNOWLEDGMENTS

A huge, heartfelt thanks goes to everyone who's supported us in our writing, especially our HUSSIES of Mountain Men of Mustang Mountain patrons:

Jackie Ziegler

To learn more about the Mountain Men of Mustang Mountain on Patreon, visit us here: https://www.patreon.com/MatchOfTheMonth

Holiday, Texas Series

All-American Cowboy

Cowboy Christmas Jubilee

Cowboy Charming

The Love Vixen Series

Getting Lucky in Love

Standalone Romances

All I Wanna Do Is You

ALSO BY EVE LONDON

Lonestar Riders MC Series*

One Night Series*

Matched with a Mountain Man Series**

Claimed by a Cowboy Series**

Summer Lovin' Series

Shared Series

July is for Jonas - Mountain Men of Mustang Mountain

May is for Mack - Mountain Men of Mustang Mountain

March is for Miles - Mountain Men of Mustang Mountain

Curvy Cheeky Charmer* - The Galentine's Chronicles Series

Crushing on a Cowboy* - Everything's Bigger in Texas Series

January is for Jackson - Mountain Men of Mustang Mountain

One Night with a Diver* - Love on the Sunshine Coast Series

Hot Diggity Dogs* - Love at First Bark Series

Hot Drummer Summer* - Hot HEA Summer Series

One Night with a SEAL* - SEAL Team Romeo

Mustard Been You* - Sycamore Mountain Man of the Month Club

Hearts on Fire* - Hearts, Flames, and Hoses Series

Beaded by Midnight* - World's Biggest Party Series

Romancing the Quarterback* - Galentine's Getaway Series

Dating the Cowboy* - Matchmakers, Inc. Series

Kiss Off Countdown* - Midnight Kisses Series

Codename: Wolf* - Soldiers for Christmas Series

Room Twenty-Four - Club Sin Series

Dangerous Curves* - Curvy Soulmates Series

Trick or Tequila** - Halloween Steam Series

Single Dad Dilemma - Starlight Bay Series

* Features one of Mama Mae's boys as the hero

** Ties to one of Mama Mae's boys

ABOUT DYLANN CRUSH

USA Today bestselling author Dylann Crush writes contemporary romance with sizzle, sass, heart and humor. A true romantic, she loves her heroines spunky and her heroes super sexy. When she's not dreaming up steamy storylines, she can be found sipping a margarita and searching for the best Tex-Mex food in the Upper Midwest.

Dylann co-hosts Romance Happy Hour (https://www. romancehappyhour.com/) with live episodes every 2nd and 4th Thursday of each month and is the founder of Book Box Babe (https://www.BookBoxBabe.com) where readers can find hand-curated, romance novel themed subscription boxes, and specialty items.

Although she grew up in Texas, she currently lives in a suburb of Minneapolis/St. Paul with her unflappable husband, three energetic kids, a clumsy Great Dane, a lovable rescue mutt, a very chill cat, and a crazy kitten. She loves to connect with readers, other authors and fans of tequila.

You can find her at www.dylanncrush.com.

facebook.com/dylanncrush

instagram.com/dylanncrush

pinterest.com/dylanncrush

bookbub.com/authors/dylann-crush

goodreads.com/DylannCrush

tiktok.com/@dylanncrush

ABOUT EVE LONDON

When Eve London was a girl she wanted to be a trapeze artist. Instead, she grew up to be like most women—a juggler—trying to keep bunches of balls in the air.

Now she spends her days writing about the kind of men she likes – sexy, shameless, and just a little bit sarcastic.

www.EveLondonAuthor.com

facebook.com/evelondonauthor

instagram.com/evelondonbooks

bookbub.com/authors/eve-london

Printed in Great Britain
by Amazon